Dear Parent:
Your child's love of reading starts h

Every child learns to read in a different way and at his or
speed. Some go back and forth between reading levels and
favorite books again and again. Others read through each lev
order. You can help your young reader improve and become
confident by encouraging his or her own interests and abilities.
books your child reads with you to the first books he or she re
alone, there are I Can Read Books for every stage of reading:

SHARED READING
Basic language, word repetition, and whimsical illustratio
ideal for sharing with your emergent reader

BEGINNING READING
Short sentences, familiar words, and simple concepts
for children eager to read on their own

READING WITH HELP
Engaging stories, longer sentences, and language play
for developing readers

READING ALONE
Complex plots, challenging vocabulary, and high-interest topics
for the independent reader

ADVANCED READING
Short paragraphs, chapters, and exciting themes
for the perfect bridge to chapter books

I Can Read Books have introduced children to the joy of reading
since 1957. Featuring award-winning authors and illustrators and a
fabulous cast of beloved characters, I Can Read Books set the
standard for beginning readers.

A lifetime of discovery begins with the magical words "I Can Read!

Visit www.icanread.com for information
on enriching your child's reading experience.

For Peggy Parish,
and cat lovers everywhere
—H. P.

To John and Brian
—L. S.

Watercolor and black pen were used to prepare the full-color art. The text type is Times.

HarperCollins®, ☕®, and I Can Read Book® are trademarks of HarperCollins Publishers.

Library of Congress catalog card number: 2007019461
ISBN 978-0-06-084351-9

Typography by Sean Boggs   ❖   Originally published by Greenwillow Books, an imprint of HarperCollins Publishers, in 2008.

Amelia Bedelia and the Cat

story by Herman Parish

pictures by Lynn Sweat

HarperCollins*Publishers*

Mrs. Rogers was in a total tizzy.

"I am late for a lunch date," she said.

"But I must find an umbrella before I go.

They say it is going to rain

cats and dogs."

"Goody!" said Amelia Bedelia.

"We will get a free pet.

Would you like a dog or a cat?"

"Neither one," said Mrs. Rogers.

"All I want is an umbrella."

"Here you go," said Amelia Bedelia.

She pulled an umbrella out of her purse.

"Why do you keep it in there?"

asked Mrs. Rogers.

"Blame Mr. Rogers," said Amelia Bedelia.

"He always tells me to save for a rainy day,

but an umbrella would be more help than money.

Would you like to borrow my rubber boots

and rain hat, too?"

"Save them for next time," said Mrs. Rogers.

"Thanks for lending me your umbrella."

7

They walked out to the car.

Mrs. Rogers got in.

"I have to go shopping later," said Amelia Bedelia.

"Really?" said Mrs. Rogers. "I may run into you."

"I hope not," said Amelia Bedelia.

"It would hurt if you ran into me."

"I have an idea," said Mrs. Rogers.

"Why don't I give you a lift

and drop you in town?"

"I know why not," said Amelia Bedelia.

"It's because I am too heavy for you to lift.

You would drop me before we got to town."

Mrs. Rogers nodded, smiled, and drove away.

Amelia Bedelia walked back to the house.

She stood on the porch

and gazed at the clouds.

"Rain cats and dogs," she said to herself.

"The weatherman might be right.

That cloud looks like a dog.

That one looks like a really big cat."

"Yipes!" hollered Amelia Bedelia

as she jumped back in shock.

"That cloud just meowed at me."

Amelia Bedelia looked down,

where the sound had come from.

MEOW... MEOW...

"Hmmm," said Amelia Bedelia.

"I have heard of a plant called a cattail,

but I've never seen a plant with a cat tail."

A kitten peeked out from behind the plant.

"Well, I'll be!" said Amelia Bedelia.

"You are the tiniest kitten

I have ever seen."

The kitten leaped out of the flowers.

It walked over to Amelia Bedelia

and rubbed up against her leg.

11

"Where's your mama?"

asked Amelia Bedelia.

"You are much too little

to be out on your own."

She picked up the kitten.

"You look like a tiny tiger,"

said Amelia Bedelia.

She scratched it between its ears.

The kitten purred and purred.

"You even sound like a tiny tiger,"

said Amelia Bedelia.

"So Tiger is what I'll call you."

She took Tiger into the kitchen.

She poured milk into a saucer.

Tiger lapped it up right away.

"Wow," said Amelia Bedelia.

"You must have been starving."

She offered the kitten

half of her sandwich.

Tiger turned up his nose.

"I need help," said Amelia Bedelia.

"I have never taken care of a cat before."

Amelia Bedelia got out the phone book.

"Aha," she said as she dialed the number.

"These folks know all about animals."

A man answered the phone and said,

"City Zoo, Mr. Lyon speaking."

"This is amazing,"

said Amelia Bedelia.

"I have never spoken with a lion."

"I am not a lion," said Mr. Lyon.

"Of course not," said Amelia Bedelia.

"I am sure that you tell the truth."

"I always do," he said.

"May I help you?"

"I hope so," said Amelia Bedelia.

"I've got a very hungry Tiger

right here in my kitchen."

"Run!" said Mr. Lyon.

"Get out of the house!"

"Calm down,"

said Amelia Bedelia.

"My Tiger is very happy.

I just gave him some milk."

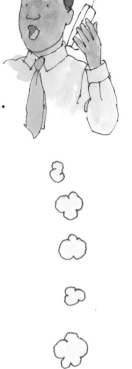

15

"Milk?" said Mr. Lyon.

"Big cats eat meat."

"You do?" said Amelia Bedelia.

"Not me," said Mr. Lyon.

"I am a vegetarian."

"You can't be," said Amelia Bedelia.

"You're a lion."

"I am not lying!" said Mr. Lyon.

"I hope not," said Amelia Bedelia.

"I have a hungry Tiger in my lap."

"Ha!" said Mr. Lyon.

"I think *you* are lying."

"No, sir," said Amelia Bedelia.

"You are a lion. I am Amelia Bedelia."

"Arrrrrgggggh!" roared Mr. Lyon.

The phone went *click.*

"Oh, well," said Amelia Bedelia.

"That lion was not much help at all.

Next time I'll ask for Mr. Tiger."

The kitten still looked hungry.

"Come along," said Amelia Bedelia.

"Let's go do our shopping.

Maybe I can find you something

to eat at the store."

CLICK!

She tucked Tiger into her purse,

locked the door, and headed into town.

Along the way Amelia Bedelia

met a letter carrier delivering packages.

"Good afternoon," he said.

"It looks like you are delivering cats."

"Oh, no," said Amelia Bedelia.

"I am trying to deliver lunch

to this hungry kitten."

"You are in luck," said the letter carrier.

"A new fish market just opened.

All cats love to eat fish."

"Where is it?" said Amelia Bedelia.

"You can't miss it," he said.

"Just follow your nose."

"Thank you," said Amelia Bedelia.

As she walked she said to herself,

"Those are very strange directions.

I follow my nose everywhere I go,

unless I walk backward."

Amelia Bedelia strolled by

Mrs. Wagner's house.

Her yard was filled with all sorts of things.

"Hi, Amelia Bedelia," said Mrs. Wagner.

"Come and take a look at my garage sale."

"No thanks," said Amelia Bedelia.

"I do not need to buy a garage.

But do you have anything for cats?"

"I did," said Mrs. Wagner.

"I just sold a litter box."

"What is that?" asked Amelia Bedelia.

"Every cat needs one," said Mrs. Wagner.

"That is where a cat goes

when it needs to go."

"Go where?" said Amelia Bedelia.

"Where would Tiger have to go?"

"Go to the bathroom," said Mrs. Wagner.

"Oh," said Amelia Bedelia. "I see.

Where would I find a litter box?"

"Let me think," said Mrs. Wagner.

"You might find one at a flea market."

Amelia Bedelia thanked Mrs. Wagner.

She kept walking toward town.

"I would not go to a flea market," she said.

"I do not want Tiger to get fleas."

Finally, Amelia Bedelia and Tiger

arrived in town.

"Look, Tiger," said Amelia Bedelia.

"We are in luck. Here is an empty box

and lots of litter, and it is all free!"

She set the box on the ground.

She filled it up with litter.

She put Tiger in the box.

"You do not look very happy,"

Amelia Bedelia said.

"I am not happy," said a voice behind her.

"Lady, what do you think you're doing?"

"I am all done," said Amelia Bedelia.

"I made a litter box for Tiger."

"You made a mess," said the policeman.

"Pick that up or I will give you a ticket."

Amelia Bedelia tossed the litter

back in the bin.

"Thank you," said the policeman.

"Please do not break any more laws."

"I try not to break things,"

said Amelia Bedelia.

She and Tiger walked on.

Tiger found the fish market first.

He sniffed the air and licked his whiskers.

Amelia Bedelia walked up to the man

selling fish.

"Excuse me," she said.

"Could you spare some scraps

for my kitten?"

"You bet," said the man.

He put some fish on a plate.

Tiger devoured the snack.

"He sure likes it," said Amelia Bedelia.

"He certainly does," said the man.

"He is as happy as a clam."

Amelia Bedelia picked up a clam and said,

"They do not look very happy to me."

The man took the clam from her.

He took out a marker

and drew a face on the clam.

"Hold it like this," he said.

"See? That is its smile."

"Now that is one happy clam,"

said Amelia Bedelia.

She laughed and looked down at Tiger.

Tiger had followed a butterfly

into the street.

"Watch out!" screamed Amelia Bedelia.

A big truck screeched to a stop.

HONNNNNNK!

Tiger dashed to the sidewalk.

He was so scared

that he scooted up a tree.

The driver got out of his truck

to make sure that he had not hurt the cat.

"Stay put, Tiger,"

said Amelia Bedelia.

"I will rescue you."

Amelia Bedelia started to climb the tree.

"Be careful," said the driver.

"Do not go out on a limb."

"I've got to save my cat,"

yelled Amelia Bedelia.

As she reached out to grab Tiger,

Amelia Bedelia slipped

off the branch.

"Whoops!" she said.

"Hang on!" said the driver.

"I will rescue both of you.

I'll get a ladder from my truck."

Amelia Bedelia held on tightly.

Tiger climbed onto her bonnet.

Then Amelia Bedelia saw

a familiar car driving up the street.

"Amelia Bedelia!" said Mrs. Rogers.

"What on earth are you doing?"

"Hanging on," said Amelia Bedelia.

"I wish I were back on earth right now."

Mrs. Rogers drove her car

directly under Amelia Bedelia.

"Let go of the branch," she called out.

Amelia Bedelia and Tiger

dropped onto the roof of the car.

Mrs. Rogers and the driver

helped Amelia Bedelia

and Tiger get down.

Amelia Bedelia tucked Tiger

back into her purse.

"Please, miss," said the driver,

"do not let that cat out of the bag again."

"I won't," said Amelia Bedelia.

"Not until we get home."

Mrs. Rogers, Amelia Bedelia, and Tiger

got into the car and drove away.

"Good thing I ran into you,"

said Mrs. Rogers.

"I gave you a lift

and did not drop you at all."

"You are right," said Amelia Bedelia.

She told Mrs. Rogers how she found

Tiger and tried to take care of him.

"In that case," said Mrs. Rogers,

"we should stop right here."

She pulled over to the curb suddenly.

"This is a very good pet store,"

said Mrs. Rogers.

"We can find everything you need

to take good care of your cat."

"Thank you so much,"

said Amelia Bedelia.

The clerk helped Mrs. Rogers gather

everything they would need,

including a litter box.

Tiger had his eye on a toy.

"You know," said Amelia Bedelia,

"I had better walk Tiger home

before he gets into any more trouble.

The house is just a few blocks away."

"See you there," said Mrs. Rogers.

By the time Amelia Bedelia

and Tiger got back home,

they were both exhausted.

Amelia Bedelia sat down.

She took off her bonnet,

and Tiger curled up in it.

The inside was soft and warm.

Tiger purred once.

A second later, he was snoozing.

"Good idea," said Amelia Bedelia.

"I will close my eyes, too,

for a minute."

She put her feet up and leaned back.

Twenty minutes later,

Mr. Rogers came home.

"Well, well," said Mr. Rogers.

"Look what the cat dragged in."

Amelia Bedelia woke up with a start.

"I am sorry," said Amelia Bedelia.

"I must have dozed off."

"Don't worry," said Mr. Rogers.

"Catnaps are nice, especially with a cat."

Amelia Bedelia introduced

Mr. Rogers to Tiger.

"Say," asked Mr. Rogers,

"where is Mrs. Rogers?"

"The last time I saw her,"

said Amelia Bedelia,

"she was in the pet store."

"Oh, really,"

said Mr. Rogers.

"My wife was in the pet store?

How much did they want for her?"

Mr. Rogers began to chuckle.

Just then, Mrs. Rogers stormed in.

"I heard that!" she said.

"Just kidding, my pet," said Mr. Rogers.

He helped her with her packages.

"Is all this for the cat?" he asked.

"Yes it is," said Mrs. Rogers.

"I should have gotten you a collar,

since you are now in the doghouse."

Mr. Rogers was not laughing now.

"Just kidding, my pet," said Mrs. Rogers.

They leaned over together

to look at Tiger.

"Who meowed?" said Amelia Bedelia.

"Don't look at me," said Mr. Rogers.

They all turned around.

A large cat sat outside the window.

It looked like Tiger, but bigger.

MEOW-MEOW-MEEEEOWWW!

Tiger sprang onto the windowsill.

Both cats were happy

to see each other.

"How sweet," said Mrs. Rogers.

"That cat must be his mother."

41

Amelia Bedelia let Tiger outside.

The big cat licked Tiger twice,

then picked him up in her mouth.

She headed across the yard.

"Stop!" shouted Amelia Bedelia.

"That big cat is eating my kitten!"

"No it isn't," said Mr. Rogers.

"That is how a mother cat

moves her babies from place to place."

They all ran after the cat.

Down the street, a moving van

was parked in front of a house.

A little girl stood in the front yard.

"What's going on?" said Amelia Bedelia.

"Is this another garage sale?"

The cat dropped Tiger into a box.

"There you are!" said the girl.

"Is that your cat?" asked Amelia Bedelia.

"Yes, it is," said the girl.

"Her name is Muffin.

My name is Sarah."

They all introduced themselves to Sarah.

Then they looked into the box.

Tiger was playing

with his brothers and sisters.

Sarah hugged Amelia Bedelia and said,

"Thanks for finding my kitten."

"My pleasure," said Amelia Bedelia.

"Is this a litter box?"

Sarah laughed. "No," she said.

"This isn't her litter box,

but this is her litter.

Muffin had kittens a month ago."

Amelia Bedelia shook her head,

shrugged her shoulders, and said,

"I still have a lot to learn about cats."

Big drops of rain began to fall.

"Uh-oh," said Mr. Rogers.

"The weatherman guessed right for once."

"Bye-bye, Sarah," said Amelia Bedelia.

"Come back tomorrow," said Sarah.

They ran back home in a downpour.

Mr. and Mrs. Rogers went inside.

Amelia Bedelia stayed out on the porch.

She looked at the rain and said to herself,

"The weather forecast was half right.

Today it only rained cats."

A tail was sticking out from behind a tree.

"Jeepers!" said Amelia Bedelia.

"A tree just barked at me."

A puppy peeked out

from behind the trunk.

It ran onto the porch

and jumped into Amelia Bedelia's arms.

"Hi there," she said. "You are soaked.

Let's go inside and dry you off."

Amelia Bedelia opened the door

and called out:

"Yoo-hoo, Mr. Rogers—

I found the other half

of the weather forecast.

Now you'll have company

in the doghouse!"

WOOF!